Molly

loved

Zehra Hicks

the girl who loved WELLIES

Macmillan Children's Books

Wellies!

She loved them so much, she wore them all the time.

In the bath . . .

On the beach . . .

Even in bed.

She never took them off!

And no one could make
her wear anything else.

One day,
Molly had
a big
itch right
in between
her toes.

just here

She tried to scratch it,
but she couldn't reach.

So she tried her umbrella . . .

and the vacuum cleaner.

Even the dog tried to help.

But the itch wouldn't go away.

There was only one
thing left to do . . .

Molly pulled . . .

and pulled . . .

and pulled.

EVERYBODY

PULLED!

Molly loved her new toes so much . . .

That now she only wears . . .

flip-flops!

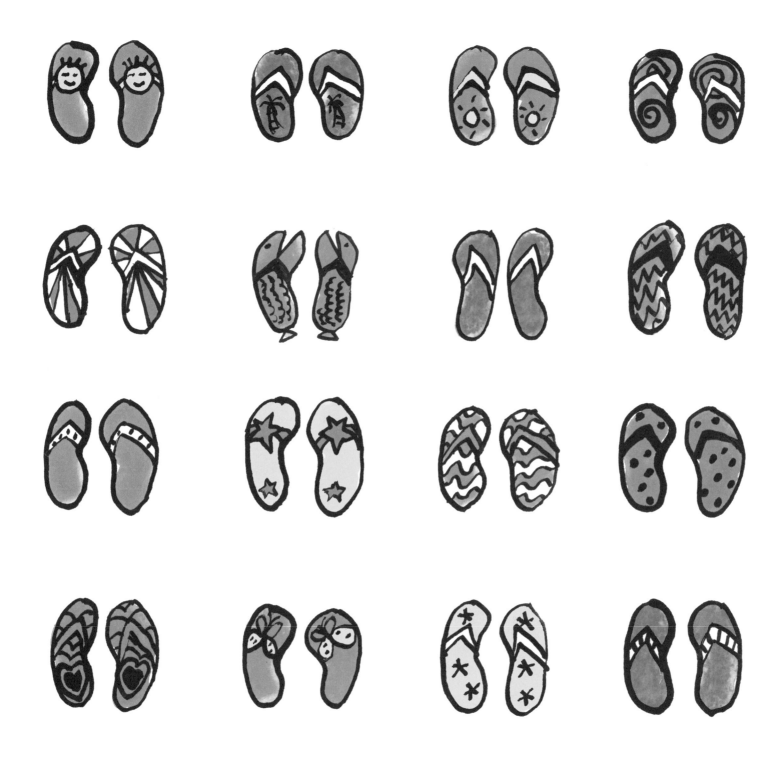